Cottonlandia

Cottonlandia
Poems

Rebecca Black

University of Massachusetts Press
Amherst and Boston

Copyright © 2005 by University of Massachusetts Press
Printed in the United States of America

LC 2004030707
ISBN 1-55849-491-X

Designed by Sally Nichols
Set in Electra LH
Printed and bound by Sheridan Books, Inc.

Library of Congress Cataloging-in-Publication Data

Black, Rebecca.
Cottonlandia : poems / Rebecca Black.
p. cm.
"Winner of the 2004 Juniper Prize for Poetry."
ISBN 1-55849-491-X (pbk. : alk. paper)
1. Southern States—Poetry. I. Title.
PS3602.L32524C68 2005
813'.6—dc22
2004030707

British Library Cataloguing in Publication data are available.

Thanks

Thanks to my first teachers, Peter Cooley and David Wojahn, to Alyce Miller, Maura Stanton, Kevin Young, David Roderick, Robin and Keith Ekiss, Ken Fields, Eavan Boland, Simone Di Piero, Louise Glück, Jonathan Hillman, Wayne Brown, Sandy Cohen, and Julia Brashares. Heartfelt thanks to Sylvain Carton and his family. And to Simeon Berry for his friendship, graceful insight, and hours of careful reading. Thanks to my family, especially to my father, Eugene Black, Jr., and my grandmother, Frances Black, for their encouragement and never-ending support.

This book would not have been possible without the support of the Wallace Stegner fellowship and residencies at Ledig House in upstate New York and at the Cité Internationale des Arts in Paris. Thanks to Madame Brunau in Paris and the Dean of the Humanities at Stanford.

Several poems from *My Only Golem* are the basis and text for a short film, *Mephista*, by the artist Erich Weiss.

Acknowledgment is made to the following magazines where these poems first appeared, sometimes in earlier versions: *Conjunctions Online* ("Mephista Recounts Her Past Lives, or Nanotechnology" and "The Legs of the Countess"); *Pleiades* ("Notes on the Tapestry of the Apocalypse"); *Virginia Quarterly Review* ("The Branded Hand of Captain Walker, Abolitionist" and "Midwestern Raptures," which also appeared at *Poetry Daily*); *Poetry* ("Cottonlandia"); *Bellingham Review* ("Showing #5" and "Vacation"); *The Missouri Review* ("1790," "Hiding the Silver," "Hand-Me-Downs," "Stomp Dancing," "Bartram Among the Seminoles," and "Bartram's Ghost"); *Notre Dame Review* ("Volterra with Two Lines from Campana"); *Southern Poetry Review* (Showing #1).

What you see as lost, set down as lost.
—Catullus

Contents

3. My Only Golem

Cottonlandia

Cottonlandia

Little wheel
something gnarls in the blood
in our Arcadia of mayflies.

We make wine from muscadines,
little wheel turning inside my heart.
In January after the crop

floats to Apalachee
other cargo arrives—old men
boot-blacked before the auction block.

Shawl of cassimere, calamus-
root, one small revolver
on offer at Muse & Co.

Little wheel turning, gossypium
grows gossypium grows
along the roads.

Cotton alone does not spin
into cloth   the bridge itself
does not burn   little wheel

turning inside my heart
what's been must be storied
grist mill   cotton gin

what's invented   inventoried

1. Photographica

The manufacture of dolls was inspired by a young woman: very much
enamoured of a man, she drew his shadow on the wall as he slept;
then her father, charmed by the extraordinary likeness—he worked with
clay—sculpted the image by filling in the contours with earth.

—Athenagoras

Wakulla Springs

I found me a cranny of perpetual dusk,
mastadon tusk, burnt wood
at spring bottom.
I dragged down low
the parts of myself
I couldn't carry,
thought to burn
those diaries as catfish
whiskered my thighs.
In the lodge, visitors
dripped aqua-blue
over marble floors,
ate canned cherries,
potatoes cut into a face.
The anhinga flapped
furred wings.
I kept down low
thought to burn
my tick-bitten breast,
every creature
crossing my chest.
Hydrilla choked the swamp.
Rivers merged
and said no more
thus the black lagoon.
I don't suppose
you knew dearest
among eel-light
and daggered palms
I made you mine by
perishing I meant to shine.

On Cumberland

When we go to the island,
I'm a native salvaging ingots
and iron bells from the wreck,

kid Caliban in poncho and sandals.
We might have set driftwood
and weeds into a quick mosaic,

or buried my brother up to his eyes
in the sand, starfish hardening
into their own caskets at his feet

so that he could be born again
from mud and sawgrass.
Coastline battered by memory—

the steel baron's fire-ruined
manor was our refuge
from a storm even the wild

horses couldn't weather.
The first sailors hurricaned
on this risen Atlantis

covered native women in moss
woven into a delicate mail
for decency's sake, bartered

deerskin for mirrors
which warriors wore
like medals or garlands

around their necks.
Imagine only seeing yourself
in the dark pupils of your mother

as she tethers your hair
in ragged linen,
then the hammered tin confusion

of a separate self.

Vacation

A bat got caught in my mother's black
bathing suit as it hung on the line.

The bat was a breast, her fluttering
heart, then a lump in the belly,

beating mound between
the legs, each chirping set

of lips, statue in which
a woman's genitalia

and mouth are reversed.
I watched from inside as waves

transmitted through fabric,
little mites rode

in the bat's fur,
parasitic as children.

Then the bat flew through
an armhole and the suit was quiet,

vacant. If a way out existed,
so did a way to touch her again.

Studies from Life

after Lady Hawarden's (1822–1865) photographs of her daughters

I keep a cabinet of dolls
nesting in shoebox cribs, a house
in miniature, wire chandelier.

Mother's brush backed
with silver—a tarnished whale
on the dresser. My hands like hers

threading through hair.
I might walk through the wall,
Clementina, while you powder

the mole on your clavicle.
You cherish that black slur.
Myself uncorsetted spilling through

the seams. You won't tell.
I jam my dolls, my ministers,
back in their dusty beds.

Some evenings
we are never put down.
The world's Girl strips us

to our slips. And forgets
to shut our eyes, leaves us
face down in the dark.

Mother's coughing
from the chemicals—her throat latches
on air, a broken clasp—

as we devise another scene:
On Affliction Beauty waits. You're A.
and I'm B. for the full exposure.

Take this night-blooming orchid
for a pelt, midnight's smooth tail
as your only interlocutor.

The ghost of a hand as Mother
unscrews the lens cap. Daughters
of Collodion, chlorine sistered,

she would never usher us
into abstraction, flesh of her
flesh. See my earrings like spears

and beads black as the spider-
selves we swept from the house's
bare corners? Sister,

let's hide beneath this veil.

The Legs of the Countess
after photographs of the Countess Castiglione (1837–1899)

Play your hand, Madame.
    Black stripe down
your dress, keyhole slit,
    door to a dark room.

If you're a pawn, why not play
    it up in kohl,
the camera your consort
    and consolation.

Queen of Hearts,
    holding a switch-
blade bouquet.
    And the Hermit

of Passy. Society pages said: *Carmelite*
    of Beauty, she retreated
into herself rather
    than retreating into God.

You rolled in glue and feathers
    to be plucked
clean by your courtiers.
    That's how it feels, Honey,

desire's a sticky bird.
    Beauty means not being,
stage-managing absence.
    Mascara's an Italian wand

for waning eyes. Your arsenic gaze—
    the gentle moth wings

a poison semaphore
    in your shuttered suites.

You did not go with grace.
    Your chalky calves,
long toes shaped
    and dyed like marzipan.

You wrote a treatise on Beauty;
    your makeup tips. And died.
No one could recall
    the color of your eyes.

Notes on the Early Heliographers

Begin in the erotic,
an outlook littered by light.
Then bellows, snowshoes

like wicker wings. The lattice
window admitted nothing
beyond the fact of lattice,

needles x'ed over glass.
Silver salts and sodium
chloride, the first photos

rose from alchemy,
as the known world doubles
when a kid casts a leaf

by light, a technique
called *innocence*. Before
the felled trees, before theories

about the city's disease,
the meter's calibration of sadness.

﹡

Who'll win the vanishing race?

1.
A man worn
in the belly of a bear
becomes the bear's innards
and secret heart. The bear fathers
the man with black fur.

2.

A stance
I haven't worn in years,
ancestral dress with bustle
and black beads, girl
clutching a gift
from the Seminoles
to my grandmother—spun
horsehair doll, kernel
eyes, given no name.
She disintegrates each time
I unwrap her striped rags.

＊

The Parable of the Documentary Photographer

Instead of firing the flash with a pistol as was my practice, I ignited
the powder in a frying pan held over head. I didn't want to disturb
the inmates, all beggars, but meant to make the process more famil-
iar, more domestic. *Twice I set fire to the house with this apparatus,
and once to myself. I blew the light from my own eyes on that occa-
sion, and only my spectacles saved me.*

＊

How bodies glue and hinge—

Plato's four-legged hermaphrodite
turns cartwheels.

In the mirror you and I
in dauguerrotypes on collodion on

the screen. Each new medium
inaugurated with flesh

airbrushed white
like the statue of the "beautiful" slave,

marble colored by the oil
of every touch.

The silent reel stutters
I hate and I love

as the photographer advances behind the plumed bride.

＊

The Branded Palm of Captain Walker, Abolitionist, c. 1844

I trace pencil lead over
the photograph—the brand follows
his life lines, a giant "M,"

and the man lives again
in indelible harm,
his hand raw in mine.

What help across the river?
Scar rising in the belly's
mark, in the tide's

happening again. Scar
like Rilke's "clearly shining 'M'"
in the stars—

which stood for "mother,"
but I call "mercury."
Poison precedes the image;

poison's mother to us all—
the first photo was light arrested
by mercury.

Without this element,
the image never ends
and thus disappears.

Have faith in poison,
wrote the traveler.
If I move faster

than the shutter, I was never here.

Showing #1

My room was snug as an anchoress' cell,
a chorus of one with cot, window set
with rocks from the quay and pasture,
a flame heather, tortoise shell.

I thought I was no one's child, lover
of none. Every village wants a solitary.
Winds down from the north met in my bones,
I slept on a nest of thistles, thorns, not knowing

we are kept alike in wealth or woe.
A deer came to the winter garden,
nosed the hellibore beneath the snow.
I thought we are half in hell,

that sin exists only in its effect,
and walked the raw corridors contemplative.
Today, stepping into the marsh,
I felt the yellow core, the divine corona.

What did I see in the field
                but light, the other shore,
the wound of a willful longing toward?

Midwestern Raptures

Black mite over the page, furious meander
      of a period untethered.
Black ant over my toes
          lifts by chambers like a lock.

Simple hydraulics, says my friend Simeon,
      out-hauling the ineffable.
Water is not water.
         That's how He walked His walk.

Faith works by metaphor, carnivorous.
     The bread is flesh;
stones are "fleeced with moss"
        and therefore sheep

in Wordsworth's example,
      and can't be parsed into tenor or vehicle.
The light of the moon is the light of the sun.
       You can't unfasten shine—

ride whatever arrives.
     Bird shits not an inch from me.
Something in that tree wants in on this story.
       The book's open so the mite

and ant alight while we doze at the feet
     of the Savior among collegial tulips.
Enter Girl with Flashcard—*What is religion?*
      An almost feasible question

the day before graduation.
     What's copied on the other side?
We'll rise like insect apostles, I pray,
      dispel our scrawlings and all false gospels

to meet in the sweet by and by
          where we go without saying.

Volterra with Two Lines from Campana

I know every swerve on the road
                 to the citadel, how light hides in cedars,

that the wind in your hair was easterly,
                 though I've never been there.

I can turn the sky into the sea, ultra-
                 marine, or say you don't love me.

Our old poet, the Tuscan pyromaniac,
                 saw *grasses burn in the graveyard with*

a pale red-ochre flame. I can get it
                 all wrong. Poor Rosso, suicidal as he painted

grief's entourage in the *Descent,*
                 Magdalene's dress like a flame or gash.

I'm not into pain, but its after-
                 math. Last night I held the ladder against the cross,

rubbed oil into the body brought
                 down, dried it with my hem, *my red and ancient heart.*

Showing #5

Each page
steals the bones of the page
before. I've dispersed

into a puddle of light
on the brown floor, studied
Melancholy, Chapter Two:
Concentrate on items you can't

hammer flush. While I slept
the skeleton key's hieroglyph
printed on the wax of my skin.
My delphinium, hear

the needle trip on *Spring.*
Spring can really hang you up
the most. I splinter a ruler over
my thighs. Slivers bloom

back into tree, painted numbers
return to ink, the beetle's body
before being crushed.
Who can tell—my chest,

this sarcophagus might fold
back into flesh. I've seen
a snake sleeping between here

and the sea, between dune
and reed like a suture.
Someone's scar might finish mine.

Notes on the Tapestry of the Apocalypse

Look how the loop of blue becomes the eye,
lasso of gray-black hair, eye lash and lash.
Nothing's better than waking up with you.

Cloud descending anvil,
anvil descending cloud.
Moti mentali:

In the dream my father was almost blind,
but he saw entire terrains, maps he'd made
of maps in the whorl of the wooden door.

I don't know how to pray—
I let the floor hold me,
don't ask for more.

         *

In the painter's early work, violence bled awkwardly.
Women and men abducted each other.
Later Cézanne agreed with the others—

there is no true black. With you,
I felt tempered, the saxophone's bell
hammered smooth. I wasn't sure

if I liked this, but I knew
in manufacturing there is a wrong side
from which the work itself must be carried out.

         *

In the tapestry, the miserable sedge
is rendered apart from the lowland sedge.
The lilacs of one coast

are not the lilacs of the other.
Some of us will be systematically terrified,
some of us soothed. Scan that

and the "hieroglyphic suffering" of some faces—
we are not the same from left to right.
I followed the disfigured through the city,

mothers and fathers made themselves
into ghosts. Listen, certain people are given to us.
We don't get to choose.

        *

Some afternoons the dragonflies hovering
outside the hospital, just the existence
of the tapestry kept me alive.

Of the destroyed cities,
a few overturned buildings remained.
Summaries of each apocalypse scene

had been misplaced. I remembered
that the sewing of any history
is synecdoche,

leavening the only legible path.
"Blessed is he that readeth
and they that hear."

        *

It was hard to distinguish afflictions,
the physical from the moral, after
the man I knew as my father died.

Hereafter, sorrow lives at the center
of the scene. Dear Reader. Dear Reader.
Death rides the prettiest things.

Everyone touches you with gloves,
punches you with gloves.
Take them off, please.

Bartram's Ghost

(The naturalist William Bartram traveled through south Georgia in 1775.)

The skies, they are beaten back,
Bartram the younger snagged in the briers

swarmed by gnats he's termed *Ephemera*,
with hope. Yucca veins the borrow pits

("borrow" a corruption of barrow)
like the tongue's other side.

While he dozes under the hornbeam,
chokeberry pulp tissued firm as the heart

stains his ankles and knees.
The tail of the glass snake splinters

by a gentle stroke from a slender switch,
and another generates

as a word gone over and over
in the mind, *tenetke*, meaning thunder,

ruptures into letter. The next morning
he finds a downed roebuck.

The hunter appears, an *Indian agent*
who barters on the invisible, also

gunpowder and skins. Bartram
knows Creek, the patois for "stream."

They share a draught
of sassafrass tea, venison and honey.

*

Under the jasmine, beyond the canebrake,
a settlement of Pleasure.

I've built a fort from the alphabet,
its scattered letters. The bulleted chamber

of the -ologists is locked, combination and chain
droop across dirt hardpacked and rutted

since the last storm.
The borrow pit sleeps in blue tarp.

The hornbeam blurs into a stand
of planted pine, two hundred years.

Description makes the world
disappear.

The mind conjures a field of feeding deer,
the sound of a stream

running through dagger palms,
pure supposition.

Bartram Among the Seminoles

Men sit in the hot house until stacked
spirals of cane burn back into carbon—

they know the time when nothing's left
to tell it by. There are drawings of men

with the heads of turkey and bear,
and drawings of animals with the heads

of men. In the granary, a mouse sleeps
in the jaws of a rattlesnake,

it has been so charmed. Bartram's clearly
lost, dreaming on pine needles

where the swamp turns into a stream.
I think he crossed the River Flint

where magnolia leaves stiff as parchment
fall to asphalt in a small town I've come

to consider cursed, though I am not prone
to superstition, only the occasional lapse

from reason or sly embellishment.
Where city fathers drained municipal pools

so the races would not commingle.
And the most peaceable creatures

are flayed, each in its own season.

*

The hunting camp's gambrel hook swings
like a new letter in the alphabet,

character in a gothic syllabary. In the creek
beside the camp of red-necked augurs,

my father's seen crawfish big as lobsters
feeding on guts. If anything keeps us

from spinning into chaos it's the swamp
De Soto called "Toa" as he slunk through

in the 1550s. Mud can cure entropy—
I've plastered it on my chest and risen up

gargantuan from the pits. Once a rattlesnake
stretched clear across the road,

and I felt the tire-thump over its belly
in my own tailbone. The snake kept going

into the cane. Better not to have bones
if you're in danger of being crushed.

Better to stay low and cultivate a presence.
The last time I was home there was a drought,

and really no reason for Oglethorpe Bridge,
so I drove back from where I'd come,

towards the smell of burning grass
in the new developments, where recent immigrants

rake embers on a lawn, paint melting
off the tines. From one window

there's a dry lake, and my father sits
with his back to the scene, his fingers gnarled

into flower buds by a stroke. My description
is half hope, half irony. Bartram knew

that naming was a misguided enterprise.
No one's sure where he was during 1774.

Likewise, this is an undocumented time.
The hornbeam is one long nerve between worlds.

If Bartram didn't sleep in the woods
near my home what does it matter? No one told

the natives their enemy De Soto was dead,
his body loaded with sand and sunk

into the Mississippi, the "sire of many rivers."
You're invited anyway to fathom the publications

of this stream, the many lost volumes of mud
it took to call this land riverine.

After Bartram crossed the flooding
Flint, he had to go on alone.

His rations were low during July 1775.
Though his hand shook with hunger,

he took great care to draw a crane
he'd never seen before. In this way we depict

what we devour and dream of our fathers.
The mouse writhes in the belly of fire.

Bartram was starving and took the bird's
roasted flesh to his own, his hands

black with ink or ash—who's left to tell?

2. Invention of the Cotton Gin

. . . knee bent and body bowed to the motherdust of earth. I am asking you this morning to look down on your children with your tender eye of mercy. And I'm asking you to come by here for a little while.

—Mother Merritt, Shiloh Baptist Church, Albany, Georgia

Before the mounds outside

of town were bulldozed
and floodlights rose totemic
from the private prison grounds,
we'd dump our trove
on the porch, sift through
Depression glass, tins
of Skoal for a feathered
arrowhead. My father brought
his pistol—a boar might rush us
at the Indian pit—but mostly
we'd zing cans off a fence
that couldn't keep the dogs in,
my brother in his fringed coat,
half Texan, fresh from
grainy westerns. Streaked
powder washed from our hands
in a shallow stream run
with fool's gold and water
moccasins. When we found
a strong bit of flint, I'd puncture it
with a trowel for a leather
string, fingering the smooth head
during spelling—*pemmican,*
talisman, traveling, days
I didn't wear the locket
inscribed "F" for "Frances,"
my grandmother's name. I was
either the Sharp-Toothed, or
the girl with something to hide.
We women all had emblems—
my grandmother wore a coin
recovered from some sunken
galleon, my mother an African
sapphire until it vanished
from her wrist.

1955

My father is kept by black women whose given names
are mapped behind the Iron Curtain: Odessa and China.

He doesn't know their last names or believe
in boogeymen, since he broke *Peter and the Wolf* and slept

on the shards, as if shattering the resin circle meant
wolves wouldn't roam. To educate meant instilling fear.

Odessa found the glossy bits and kept his secret. He hums
her songs *we are climbing Jacob's ladder*

we are climbing Jacob's ladder. At six, his fears
are rational—a cloud of radiation might dissolve

the free world into dust as he sits atop the pony shed.
He doesn't log the bomber recons from the base as some

boys do. In twelve years, a cloud of dirt billows into
the sewer tunnel he's digging with his friend. The boss

thinks both boys are dead—my grandmother paces
at the site until one body is borne up on a rope. For now,

she trills *Alleluias* in the Methodist choir, says *Gardenias!*
when my father brings a runnersnake to the table.

And in Mississippi, Emmett Till, 14, formerly of Chicago,
is found with a cotton gin motor coiled to his neck

like the circling of a round.

1519 Parkview Court

The summer my mother wrote
a thesis on the brain's capacity
for conjugation, *specto, spectare,*

we took long Sunday drives,
stopped to trap snapping turtles,
saw armadillos migrating east,

reverse Conquistadors. Along
state roads, palmettos. Bronze
plaques grew on steel posts

in the clay with quotes forged
and sourceless. In our subdivision,
built on arsenic-coated cotton fields

dredged from the Flint, neighbors
campaigned to keep a black family
out. Flyers shoved under the door

warned *sinking property
values.* Saturdays, after mowing lawns,
my brother climbed shingles,

aimed at the pinking-shear crowns
of wild chickens, and punctuated
the tool shed with bird shot,

while my father waited for deer
a county over in fields burnt
after a storm. He'd bring home

sugar cane with ants encased
in syrup, wave a stalk of cotton bolls.
I wanted to win the ginning contest,

pick the seeds fastest by hand. Eli
Whitney, my primer said, was
the father of manumission. And:

*In 1837, all of this was virgin
cotton land, the last of the Creeks
were run out of town, named Albany*

*for the white beach where Aeneas
landed after the war and a visit to the dead.*
Someone down the street had

a three-fingered child, then
a tremor started in my mother's
right arm. What made us sick

among the amnesiac fields?
Evenings my father read us Du Bois:
perhaps the richest slave kingdom

the modern world ever knew. I'd go
sit in the clearing, imagine Goodman,
Schwerner and Chaney's charred

half-buried Ford discovered by Choctaws
in Mississippi, 1963. The year
my father was fifteen, National

Guardsmen mounted on the courthouse
roof saw the brown river lap
its banks, heard the refrain: *the fire*

*in the flint never shows til it's struck,
there's a fire in the Flint that won't go down.*

Sweet transmigrations

of the soul in Terrell County
swamplit matin and deer call.

In '39, Otis Redding's born
here to die in a Cessna
over a far northern field.

I want you to come back
come back I've had enough.
What offerings

to the dead, a wreath
for the ones born mewing
music, for my father

camouflaged in the field,
rifle across his knees,
reading a paperback life

of Bonhoeffer, who returned
to Germany knowing
he'd kill the dictator

or be killed. Soul of bullet
smoke, the faltering engines.
Back in our city of wells,

water runs under bare groves.
No one's as lonely as my father
as he lets the gun go

and falls asleep. At least
one living thing is spared.
Redding calls out

from beyond—
these arms of mine are yearning.
if you would

let them hold you

Talbotton County, 1923

Small god of histories, make yourself known.
Clay-eater, smith and jester, bend the dogwood

down. Tell me who cheated who at cards,
who placed spade next to heart before that ghost,

my great-great uncle, slashed a man's throat
with his penknife? And walked himself weeping

to the county jail. His nephew sent later
with a flour-sack of cash to bribe the governor

of Sugar Creek. Child of child of pocketknife
and cannon fodder, motoring past sand dunes

far below sea level, I do shadow-time,
imagining the boy sent with the bribe

made to wait all day on the capitol
steps, face burning from sun and shame.

I won't report my crimes. The murderer
my great-great uncle escaped the gallows,

married a poor woman who kept him sane.
The boy ran a cotton mill for fifty years.

As he died he told us his secret story—
saying sure you can purchase mercy sure

you can. But everything you gotta buy costs high.

Typing Lessons

A pigtail-snatching witch hid
      behind the bed and Colonel Slaughter,
         halved by a cannonball

at Chancelorsville, thumbed
      for defunct statutes in the library,
         days Mary and I opened the book

of ghosts. We hugged
      the dead close, like dolls. Shadows
         miscarried on the ceiling when

we read—girls disappeared
      down wells, hexed into changelings.
         Soon Mary's dad died fixing

a rifle jam. I didn't know
      what to say, so I said nothing. Survival
         left me wooden—the girl changed

into a tree. Colonel Slaughter's
      books turned to powder while amputees
         waited to see my father about benefits.

From the half-lives
      in files I typed at the office sometimes—
         a woman's contorted spine,

no kerosene for heat, the epileptic's
      tongue-tied litany—I might have learned
         compassion. I gummed peppermints,

fanned manila folders
on the floor. Some clients were
visited with pain, the queen of spades,

or grief, the queen of hearts.
My job was "not to interpret
but to record," so I clicked tiny tapes

into a machine and channeled
voices—someone's back snapped
in a lumberyard.

The technologies of grief, scrolled
monitor and keyboard,
green words, black screen.

Five-Hundred-Year Flood

After the '94 flood, coffins
popped up like champagne
corks in the cemetery
and the county horticulturalist
was called to graft remains
under a tent. We gathered
for the remembering, antebellum
bodies sewn together
from risen parts. Our fair
city founded in 1828, forests
stumped for mansion floors,
burned huts along the Muckalee,
the *pour-on-me*. By then
the Creeks had been removed
by Jackson's men, leaving
a pig jawbone and china shards
we tried to paste into
an actual plate.
                After the flood,
caves shifted under radium springs
under jimsonweed and moss
that fed on air. The present
a hallucination of every past
August's shimmer and tar.
The horticulturalist slept
on sinkholes—had visions
of medicine men in trees,
swamp things, and set fire
to his own trailer. For a minute
it glowed like a planetarium ball,
like the jack-o-lanterns I
joker-carved, firmaments
hacked from the rotting hollows.

Churchgoing, 1989

Paper fans given by competing
funeral homes disappeared after
the church got conditioned air.

The faithful no longer sweated
through baptisms; for the shut-ins
at home, "The Hour of Power"

broadcast from Atlanta.
After church I'd change
out of my stockings,

drive past the peach stands
to the edge of a field. I learned
to shoot a gun at a row of pines

dead down the middle,
the crop-duster's mistake.
I would be divided too, so Sundays

I ignored the sermon, listened
instead to the devices intended
for the hearing-impaired

hooked in each pew. I'd hold
one to each ear—the brown
rubber blooms like stalks of cotton

after the chemical dousing.

Doughtery County Jail

I shadowed the jailer and the women
looked through me, a ribboned apparition,
ten-year old touring the house
of corrections. *Hurts not to nurse my baby,*

I overheard, my green sash covering
the spot where I'd sew a badge.
Ten summers later I learned to waltz
with my head just-so, to bow

not to God but to fathers, to boys
with flasks stashed in stiff tuxedoes,
as the river flooded downtown.
City prisoners ballasted the courthouse

with sand, choreographed
in orange. Trailers in the flood-plain
eased from cinder foundations, gas
mains blew, and homes were as advertised,

mobile. The river would no longer accept
processionals funded by the barons
of yarn and beer, the accolades of maiden
troupes of twirlers. In college that fall,

in a state exporting leg irons to Sweden,
having watched prisoners be bucked
from bulls at the Angola rodeo, I, dumb
volunteer, scrubbed dried sewage

from a flood disaster wagon and caught
pneumonia—the past no seed, but pathogen.

Scavenger

Crowe the potter fed the kiln
with wood from old squatter shacks
for twenty-four hours at a time,

embering wares with alchemical signs
to sell at the replica plantation
Westville, "Where it's always 1849."

We'd watch the fire all evening,
seared with sweat and ash. One night
my dad slipped cash into a cup

of seeds on their kitchen counter—
melon, cucumber and plum—
while Crowe's wife showed me

a ragged photo of a Roman
fountain, her daydream. When Crowe
got mystical from the rafters, claimed

to be the seventh son of the sculptor
Lombardo, or a lesser-known
archangel sent to save derelict

Baptists, she'd call my dad to talk
him down. I waited in the kitchen
with the wife in her fur wrap,

wind through plastic-coated windows,
attic and porch bursting with bowls
Crowe spun from the very ground.

Crowe wasn't coming down
this time. He yelled he'd kick
away any ladder he'd ever climbed.

Hand-Me-Downs

My mother wore the collared, pearl-buttoned blouse
for teaching. After Caesar reached the Rubicon, *alea
jacta est*, she'd turn to the mysteries of Demeter's sorrow.

The blouse, stained with the last of a scent called Joy,
went to Ruby, into the smoke and Schlitz
of a Calhoun juke joint, where she was keyboards

Saturday night. She'd left the sewing factories to raise
her nephew in the country. She could write, but I
only saw her chalk requests for more Ajax, or pick out

a melody on our soured piano. She didn't sing. Once
I left out pennies for her, but she dusted over the pile.
A thousand Lincolns wouldn't change a goddamned

thing. When we drove twenty miles to visit—she
was sick—we took my mother's old curtains made
from bolts of blue colonial chintz. I didn't know

anything. We never spoke of more than how she took
coffee "black and sweet." Ruby knew our secrets—
how the girl bloodied sheets in her sleep, how to hold

the mother after the dose of L-Dopa. When I heard
Ruby turn the key in the lock, I'd huddle with a book
in bed until she called me to help with the towels,

to tear my father's threadbare Oxfords into rags.

Hiding the Silver

After my mother served coffee
from her reproduction Chippendale
seat, the silver service was deposited
in the sideboard with a tassled
key, or hidden in the bathtub
if we left town for a week.

This meat fork from the Colliers,
a chest of hollow ware from the Kings.
Our ancestors conjured by their ritual
tools, as if we'd always know what
to do. But my brother bent
the bone-handled knife prying open

a jelly lid, and I floated
camellias in the gravy boat.
Silver from families with no daughters
was plundered—a woman got hold
of Uncle Collier before he died
and pawned Aunt's dowry.

(She'd had no memory for years.)
We found the empty chest,
its red velvet crumbled
like dried blood in my hands.
At school, white girls wore
bracelets of silver spoons. Their wrists

blacked with tarnish, the metal
almost issued from their veins
as they collected toy trucks
and marbles for the Charity League's
Christmas stockings.

I read alone during lunch each day:

the moon and silver equal charity.
If I shined and polished
the silver service, my mother said,
my face convex in the sugar
bowl, working a rag over
the cream pitcher, cold water

beading the sheen, and my fingers
ached a sooty blue, I could give
it away when I died. She wanted
me to earn the past, her things.
But I worked in the kitchen to hear
my grandmother's stories:

Pearl's mother would be damned
if she'd surrender a twenty-dollar piece
to the Yankee soldiers who comandeered
her farm.
           She hid the gold
in her mouth and gave the unbroken
pony back to the waxing moon, saying
"If you can catch it, it's yours."

1790

Whitney forged Revolutionary nails
and hat pins, then muskets with changeable parts
when his gin patent was delayed.

Competitors arsoned his barn, stole
his plans. Still he wrote: "One man and a horse
will do more than fifty men without

throwing any class of People out
of business." Thereafter, at the cotton mills upriver
which my forebearers oversaw,

counterfeit machines pressed
cotton into bales shipped to England. Seeds
mouldered beside a great pyramid

of lint. Before the gin, a slave's shoe
full was a winter night's work. Afterwards,
gin wheels churned like Ezekiel's

and the night miller hummed
a sorrow song. "So the thirty thousand Negroes
of Georgia in 1790 were doubled

in a decade, were over a hundred
thousand in 1810, had reached two hundred
thousand in 1820, and half

a million at the time of the war," wrote Du Bois.
This capital of Cotton built on our backs.
Dear Jesus deliver us from the Egypt of the South.

De Rerum Natura

I kept the widow aunts company
      at the Rock one summer, playing
            rummy with the shades drawn.

A Seminole doll brought from the attic
      mentored me in Sawdust
            while my mother got

an advanced degree in Athens,
      studying Lucretius.
            We don't know why it happened,

but her disease started symmetrically,
      in her right hand then left,
            and she was half of me.

(According to the family, the other
      half included fool mule-traders,
            the whiskey-sodden farmer

sleeping it off during Revival,
            the one-legged veteran who sired
                  a millionaire and my father.)

That summer I read of life in the stars,
      of magic mitochondria, the past
            and future in a cell. What skeletons

would I have to swaddle, what pains
      would visit like a chain letter
            beginning "Dear Skinnyflint?"

Stomp Dancing

Summers at Chehaw Park, Cherokees
returned from western reservations
for a festival. I'd watch the stomp dance
with my brother from the bleachers,
the beer company's Clydesdale parade.
What change would dancing bring?
We bought turquoise rings, authentic
hachets, a t-shirt that read *Trail
of Tears*, while ants worked candy wrappers
and cola tabs into a mound, and the lone
buffalo at the zoo died of mange.
Our house tomb-quiet until I stomped in
past curfew, jammed out to The Wailers,
scripting silly thrillers with my Black
Warrior pencil. On weekends we'd argue
over the stereo: Dad's tapes of native
chants, opera dubbed on the other side,
or my redemption songs. One summer
Seminoles raided the diorama at Kolomoki
for their ancestors' bodies. They descended—
gods from the machine—to load boxes
of bones into a Winnebago airbrushed
with eagle wings. I stood very still
in lipstick and stirrup jeans next to the wax
figures of squaw and brave
and the archaeologists, who seemed
stunned at the dismantling. The opposite
of a ceremony. Working together,
my dad whispered, each man might
bear the dead weight of ten.

3. My Only Golem

Also a little girl jumped out of my mouth with a little brown frock and a little black apron—my little daughter, she is granted to me—O God, the deputy—she is the deputy. . . I came first as a double, as sole owner of the world, first with the deaf and dumb.

—Jung, as related by Avital Ronell

My Only Golem

Cursed be the one who makes a carved or molten image,
the work of the hands of an artisan, and sets it up in secret.
—Deuteronomy

Miss Nobody, sister
twin, I bequeath red plastic
funnels for breasts, hair
from the four corners
of my bed. For your shoe
a stone that bruised
my heel, razored blood,
a dram of jealousy. I'll
mortar you with muck
from the River Flint, fixident,
a jigger of my lost
drawl. Everything
I hate about myself.
The eighteen-year fever
coiled in my bones, a hitch
in the lungs, left ear mole.
In your stomach, brick
of cornbread, capers.
For your nethers,
a mollusk shell, fly
trap, only part
of the story.
You're the ache
& the cavity. Wire
helix of hair, willow
furl rigged with polyester
thread, taffeta rags,
shredded energy bills.
I'll feather your brow

with mystical letters,
Kabbalah kitten, my
golem. Marionette,
my maker and mask,
I name you Mephista.

The Dreaming Golem

And the other selves deployed:
my pretty crime tightens
the straps on her filched
shoes. The decoy
sent downriver returns
riddled. Terrorista, bomb
taped to her heart.
My roaring girl, smoking
gun. You're inviolable, cut-
purse, my specialist
with a butter knife. This
colony stocked with ivory,
blackest of all black
inks, any adjective
I desire. My continued
debauch, I renounce
all claims & insinuation.
My duped confessor,
hanged judge.
Always comes
the recurring (*After you
dearest language*)
surrender. I've finished
your body off
with a colossal pencil
then shined my own
boots, Miss Nightmare,
caper and epic chase.
I'll flee under Venus
til apprehended.

Mephista to Miss Black

You're the girl who does know better but.
Getting so smart no man
will call, sister made
of clay like me.
Confession: I picked
the lock on your diary.
You slept
for seven years,
so I wrote this
in bubble script
on the tissued pages:
My horse comes
when called "Amnesia."
Avenger of the plagiarist
and the cheat, stunt-double
for justice, matinee idol, the idler,
your seamstress. Rollerskating,
I like to fall. I sew the dead
together, your research
assistant. Offer myself limb
by limb to this house on fire.
I do your dirty work,
Missus. I'm that wench.

Mephista Summering

In the appaloosa's ear
my Thumbelina directs
hooves by remote.
Cartoon angel formed
from clouds altered
by auto emissions.
Thus I commit
to omit all engines,
to the colony
via horsepower!
Feted by horse-
flies, bicycle rides,
jerked beef & blink,
nasturtiums
in the salad. Tagalong,
have you unpacked?
I've ironed seventy-two
appellations for you, sister
formed from the seven
days, infinite
& divisible. Let's
bless each bone depleting
bless each nerve bless
the spasm of all verbs.
Bless deer and poacher—
take it from that poor wren
pressing her breast
against each new scrap
her nest & obverse—bless
Hurt, I'm game.

Mephista as the Desert Rose

Dear girl, join the campaign
to reconsider Nevada,

its traffickers and ghost ships.
My Westward Ho, my Hwy. 50 baby.

On the loneliest road in America
in the dark

the mere flash of a lit cigarette
informs the enemy.

O the lost art of the CB.
Heart-breaker breaker one nine.

We sped through meth lab fires,
starfires of Babylon, past the plants

of jellybeans. Soot and orange dolor
in the burning desert.

    O small colors
& taste of larger tangibilities.

Mephista Recounts Her Past Lives, or Nanotechnology

Newsflash, Missus—machines
have been invented
to invent machines.
I know you depend
on me to make your name.
But before you plucked
me canopic, I peddled atoms
at the linear accelerator;
I kept myself in penny dreadfuls
by importing diction illegally.
After fencing with Herr Doctor
Faustus, after purely scientific
revelations, I came to
with this jingle:
"That's what happens/
in nuclear fusion."
Though I was orphaned
as Orpheus before you,
I'm no liar. I trawled
and groveled rather intelligently.
Adhere to these warnings, Miss B.:
If you try to remove the blemish
from my cheek by chemistry,
correct my limp by a-mal-gams
I'll dissolve and you'll be dissolute.
But like a good child,
(Edgar to Glouster)
when you de-sire,
when you want to leave
me to history
I'll take you to the edge—
what you think is the edge, is death—
watch you flounder
in the shallows. I'll hand you
the pistol after emptying the chamber.

Mephista and Miss B. in Moravia

Wearing your waxed
raincoat, blonde wig,
I followed you through
Eastern capitals, through
ticker tape avenues,
confetti spiralling like DNA
until we shared a Pepsi
under a blue umbrella
in Brno. Which once
was Austria, where pea-
vines grew wild
in the garden of Father
Mendel. (Only a celibate
was patient enough
to cross and hybridize
generations, to discover
the laws of descendency,
said Miss. B.)
Everything else
tries to keep existing.
Shadow remembers fire
its maker, fire its maker
ice. (Miss B. tries
very hard to exist.)
But Mephista means
to end the self
as a bomb's designed
to beget bomblets,
as I abandon
this mission called
Abandonment.
Fighter planes vaporize
over the peavines, over
these republics of desire.
Let denotations ripple
forth & detonate.

Chelsea Episode

My daimon accompanied me
to the Gallery Contempo—
tug & trireme, exotic flora

of blown glass displayed.
Slump and fuse, slump
and fuse—the best technique

for blowing sand into art.
If pressed, Mephista,
I'll tell you—as taxis

progressed, as prisms cross-
pollenated—I was exquisite
liquid then a hard crush

under your heel. You
were plotting a heist
until a crystal thorn

nicked your thumb.
The dear sculptor G.
asked for our review

with the word "chrysanthemum"
struck out. Like a polygraph,
he said, the pencil veered

on an invisible grid. *Axis of Conflict.*
Axis of Crisis. Did you hear
the final unravelling of pistil

and stamen as night fell?
Maybe there was no crime–
Dénouement. Maybe

the crime is we.

Seduction, or the Unicorn Tapestries

The horse makes its little
leap of nothing.
Also called the Ravishing.
I won't deny what happened.
I took from your side
the eternal. My right.
My pleasure.
Who believes in you?
Knots make this tapestry
pretty—on the wooden floor
the tangle of your under-things.
You shave your legs until
—is this—before
or after? *they gleam*
like mammoth tusks.
I didn't mean to say,
to imply that I consider
you my quarry.
Look, the fence is low.
Leap if you want to go.

Mephista as Material Witness

At approximately 2 a.m.
after Miss B. exited the realm
of antiquity, passing through
the caves of Academe,
she abandoned this draft,
termed Exhibit B:

From the burned Anatolian city,
you brought back a coral rug
where mistakes were made by hand,
the pattern's lament.
Then a premonition—archaic raiment—
Mother, you've brought a burning gown
for me to wear.

Did Miss B. undertake
familial conspiracies,
women put to rest
in wedding dresses,
women dressed
to kill? Mephista—
did Miss B. put on knowledge—
strike that—did she put on
a black sheath for the post-
lyric apocalypse? Did she throw
the mirror at herself?

Mephista at the Blackboard

constructs a genealogy.
Who was the mother
of Miss B., her grands?
The mother drew
posters detailing sperm
and ova, exhorted her
not to smoke and imbibe.
The grands taught her
to knit items of no utility.
(Let it be said they tried.)
The family—all too
nuclear. Mother hacking
quilts backed in black
from Father's ties.
And the man still
alive! Metaphors
like gin colliding
with vermouth after 5.
(O some taught biscuits,
vinegar in the greens.
Some wrote letters entirely
about the weather
truly relating cosmologies.)
Mephista, knock erasers
together on red bricks.
My brat & tabula rasa,
your lineage graffiti-
writ. Aren't you glad
to be adopted, glad
to opt out
of that cussed parentage?

Miss B., with Cotton Candy

From sugar-cloud she sees him,
son of the lion tamer—
how he commands
those wolfhounds, ignites
steel hoops, her flame!
She'll write him letters
on onion-thin air-mail
as a member of Troop
Forget-Me-Not, tier
of knots. She makes herself up
when no one's home,
shaves her legs until
they bleed and bleed.
Her current dilemma:
to live in art or join
the damned handbell
choir of humanity?
She wasn't quite missing
anything—cherry red Schwinn
bell-equipped—yet
mornings were music
on low speed, Mother
battering a cake.
And Mephista trailed,
Dublette with a KGB-issue
lipstick pistol, shoe-heel receiver.
Sole: This is Soul. Do you read?
Mother and God are not at home.
Unheimlich. That was exactly it.
Damned carillon, flaming
hoops. Her dress caught
in the spokes! The world
rings and rings.

Mephista as Roaring Girl

Lest you think me
a mere mouthpiece
for the author—I'll get
her banished and become
a B-Movie star: *Girl with the*
Laughing Eyes, Reno Tramp.
I slurp black pudding
at the altar, implore
the duck to roast
the cook, students
to thrash the teacher.
I walk the second line
with black indians,
rumpus-queen,
Moll with a megaphone,
I lead the cheers:

>"Devote yourself to beautiful trash!
>Create ceremonies of gladness
>From rituals of sadness!
>The world reverses above us,
>And all the scholars steal!"

Then my gray hair
grows thick; hens hatch
sour apples. I shrink
to the size of a newborn,
to the radius
of a pea,
disappears!

Mephista among the Surrealists

Claudie sweetens
your tea with little
packets of malice
while you entertain
on the harmonica.
Bellmer the marionettist
imagines you shaped
by his lathe, continues
to cathect. Minor
poets sentence you
to death.
If I'd been there,
baby, I'd trade my hips
for your brain while
the spoons rose up
against the pans. Lau-
danumed as a god,
strung out as a puppet,
someone (Rrose
probably) said
you didn't fit in,
like a false leg.
It was then that you
first felt shame,
and ran up fallopian
stairs leading nowhere
to arrive in my arms,
gasping that there seemed
no end to pain.
"To Pleasure," I said.

Miss B. Misses the Train

In your city of funiculars,
of staggering
turns, in your city
of drawls hydraulic
(yes'ms and no'ms),
delusions wave handletter'd
signs. In the metropolis,
something is always
being stolen, alarum
itself is commandeered.
Even you are a snatched
vehicle, vamping
in a mink stole,
searching the necropolis
for souls to galvanize.
Explicit Vaudeville.
You've lost
the same watch twice,
decided to make some time.
Before the days divided
neatly into hours
to be mined,
the nights were ours.
You wake up feeling
like you're out of time.
Nobody's arms wind
tight around your ticking.

Vegas and Environs

Dear Missus,

In the distance,
Vegas grows hydroponic
from white grit.

As an honorary daughter
of the Black Aircraft,
I've seen true alien skulls,

hypersonic vehicles,
bats crashing into
squadrons, the secret

flying machines
Sabre & Penetrator.
Dazzled by Sinatra

syncopated fountains,
Sammy Davis, Jr.
after hours at the Sands,

Moldavian trapeze artists.
(The Communists taught
contortion while America

coined its military missions
Tortuga, Diamonda,
Dauphin & Baseball.)

Missus, in response
to your questions,
pleadings, let there be

no proceedings.
I was summoned
by the universe

to hover angelic
over history instead
of hoovering your carpet.

There is an infinite disorder
which takes precedence
over washing the collards

or buttering your toast.
I shall be gone
for some time, Miss B.

I trust that you will iron
out your own hypotheses.
Signed,

Mephista

P.S.

Expense Report:

The whole escapade
took seven tanks
of gas, a thermos
of Margaritas,
& five sandwiches of cheese.

The Renunciation of Mephista

She dances like a bomb abroad.
                    —Emily Dickinson

In the end, I wipe
the letters from your temple
and life spells
death. You sink back
to silt and mangrove.
I might give you up
for a nun, resuscitate
my man.
(I would love you
but you are too
like me.)
For now, sew
this note to your sleeve
so you know
the way home.
You've taken root
like a word, my stray.
Tell me: does imagination
begin in jealousy?
I want to make every-
thing not me
mine. Miss Metaphor,
my mute, mutt,
mutter.

Notes on the Poems

"Wakulla Springs" starts with a line by Sterling Brown. "On Cumberland" is for my brother. "Notes on the Early Heliographers" owes a debt to Sarah Burns's lectures on the history of photography and refers to the life of Jacob Riis, among others. "Showing #1" ends with a line from Julian of Norwich's *Revelations of Divine Love*. "Midwestern Raptures" is for Simeon Berry. "Volterra with Two Lines from Campana" describes paintings by Corot and Rosso Fiorentino; Dino Campana's lines are quoted from Charles Wright's translation of *Orphic Songs*. "Notes on the Tapestry of the Apocalypse," for Sylvain Carton, is based on the tapestry in Angers, France; the poem uses a phrase by Simone Weil: "hieroglyphic suffering."

"Sweet transmigrations" includes several lines from Otis Redding's "These Arms of Mine." "1790" was informed by W. E. B. Du Bois's "Souls of Black Folk."

The epigraph for *My Only Golem* is from *The Telephone Book: Technology, Schizophrenia and Electric Speech* by Avital Ronell. "After you/dearest language" in "The Dreaming Golem" is quoted from André Breton. "Mephista to Miss Black" starts with a line from John Berryman's "Of 1816." "Chelsea Episode" is for the sculptor Gary Quinonez. "Seduction, or the Unicorn Tapestries" contains two paraphrased lines from Adrienne Rich's "Snapshots of a Daughter-in-Law."

Rebecca Black lives in San Francisco and is a lecturer at Santa Clara University. She was a Wallace Stegner fellow at Stanford University, and received an M.F.A. from Indiana University in 2002. She has been a writer-in-residence at Ledig House/Art Omi in New York and at the Cité des Arts in Paris.

The
Juniper
Prize

This volume is the 30th recipient of the Juniper Prize
presented annually by the University of Massachusetts Press
for a volume of original poetry. The prize is named in honor
of Robert Francis (1901–1987), who lived for many years
at Fort Juniper, Amherst, Massachusetts.